The Legend of
Saint Christopher
Quest for a King

Written and Illustrated by
LEE Hyoun-ju

Pauline
BOOKS & MEDIA
Boston

Library of Congress Control Number: 2016958839

CIP data is available.
ISBN 10: 0-8198-4588-4
ISBN 13: 978-0-8198-4588-7

예수님을 업은 크리스토포로 (Christopher Bearing Jesus on His Back) © 2014

by LEE Hyoun-ju, www.pauline.or.kr.

Translated by Kyung Hee Yoon.

Originally published by Pauline Books & Media, Seoul, Korea. All rights reserved.

Copyright © 2017, Daughters of St. Paul for English Edition

Published by Pauline Books & Media, 50 Saint Pauls Avenue, Boston, MA 02130–3491

Printed in the U.S.A.

LOSC VSAUSAPEOILL12-1210078 4588-4

www.pauline.org

Pauline Books & Media is the publishing house of the Daughters of St. Paul, an international congregation of women religious serving the Church with the communications media.

1 2 3 4 5 6 7 8 9   21 20 19 18 17

CHAPTER 1

BIRTH OF A GIANT

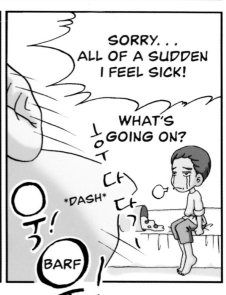

ALTHOUGH OFFERUS' MOTHER WAS CHRISTIAN, SHE WAS NOT ABLE TO RAISE HER SON IN THE FAITH. HE GREW UP TO BE VERY TALL AND WAS STRONG ENOUGH TO DO THINGS OTHERS COULD NOT. PEOPLE OFTEN ASKED FOR HIS HELP. OFFERUS FOUND THAT THE MORE HE SERVED OTHERS, THE MORE HIS DESIRE TO SERVE GREW.

GRUNT

YANK

WOW!

THAT HUGE TRUNK WAS LIKE A TWIG TO YOU!

IT WAS EASY!

FWOOSH!

SON!

SIR!

OFFERUS, CAN YOU MOVE ALL THE ROCKS IN THE RIVER TO MAKE A RESERVOIR?

YES, FATHER, I'LL BE THERE RIGHT AWAY.

YOU MUST BE SO PROUD OF YOUR SON. HE MOVED ALL THOSE ROCKS IN ONE DAY!

HIS STRENGTH AND HEIGHT ARE GIFTS FROM THE GODS.

OVER THERE, OFFERUS!

HOW WAS YOUR DAY? YOU'RE ALWAYS SO HELPFUL TO EVERYONE. IT'S GREAT!

I GUESS I ENJOY HELPING PEOPLE.

YOU'RE SO GENEROUS, OFFERUS. MANY PEOPLE ONLY THINK ABOUT THEMSELVES. YOU THINK ABOUT OTHERS.

MY MOTHER TAUGHT ME THAT I SHOULD USE MY GIFTS TO HELP OTHERS.

I'M SURE THAT THERE IS SOMEONE MORE POWERFUL THAN ME—SOME GREAT RULER OR KING.

I WANT TO FIND HIM AND SERVE HIM; THAT'S WHAT I WANT TO DO WITH MY LIFE.

GRRR!

WHAT ARE YOU WAITING FOR? FIGHT!

YOU'RE MORE OF A COWARD THAN I THOUGHT.

DEFEND YOURSELF!!

RUSH

WHAT . . . UGH, HE'S SO STRONG!

LET'S GO, OFFERUS.

OKAY.

WAIT!

I'M MAXIMUS, THE KING'S BODYGUARD. HE HAS HEARD ABOUT YOU AND WANTS TO MEET YOU. I WAS TESTING YOU TO SEE IF THE RUMORS ABOUT YOUR STRENGTH WERE TRUE.

THE KING?

I'VE NEVER BEEN DEFEATED BY ANYONE. BUT YOU WERE ABLE TO DO SO WITH ONE HAND!

A GREAT AND POWERFUL KING . . . EVERYONE ELSE IS AFRAID OF HIM.

COME AND BE THE GREAT KING'S SERVANT!

CLIP CLOP
CLIP CLOP

THE TIME HAS COME FOR ME TO LEAVE HOME.

YOU'RE GOING TO THE KING, THEN?

I'VE ALWAYS WANTED TO SERVE SOMEONE GREAT. I'VE GOT TO FIND OUT IF . . .

AND IF HE IS . . .

THIS KING IS THE ONE I SHOULD SERVE.

WILL I EVER SEE YOU AGAIN?

YOU CAN COME VISIT ME, HELENA!

OFFERUS?

WHO WILL HELP THE PEOPLE WHEN YOU LEAVE?

SOME DAY I'LL COME BACK. I'LL HELP THEN.

CREAK

HELENA!

I DIDN'T WANT TO SAY GOODBYE . . .

CAN A GIANT OF A MAN, LIKE YOU, REALLY SNEAK AWAY?

HAHA. I'LL MISS YOU.

I WANT TO GIVE THIS TO YOU.

SNIFF.

WHAT IS IT?

A SNACK FOR WHEN YOU GET HUNGRY.

OH, I HAVE SOME FOOD ALREADY.

FINE! THEN GIVE IT TO A DOG. WHY DID I BOTHER?

STOMP

HUG

IF THE KING ISN'T WHAT MAXIMUS SAYS HE IS, I'LL COME BACK AS SOON AS I CAN.

OFFERUS! I'LL PRAY YOU DISCOVER MY GOD.

HE IS THE BEST KING. NOW HURRY! THE SUN IS COMING UP AND PEOPLE WILL SEE YOU LEAVING.

SERVING AN EARTHLY KING

CHAPTER 2

THE PALACE IN CANAAN

WOW! IT'S BEEN A LONG TIME SINCE MY HEAD HASN'T HIT THE CEILING.

UNBELIEVABLE! LOOK AT HIM!

I'VE ALWAYS WANTED TO PUT MY STRENGTH AT THE SERVICE OF A TRULY POWERFUL KING. I SENSE YOU ARE GREAT. YES, I'LL SERVE YOU!

I WISH TO BE YOUR SERVANT, EVEN THOUGH I AM UNWORTHY.

BOW

WITH YOU, NO ONE WOULD EVER DARE TRY TO ATTACK US!

I PROMISE TO FAITHFULLY SERVE THE GREAT AND POWERFUL KING!

AND YOU, MY TRUSTED SERVANT, I WILL KEEP BY MY SIDE.

CLAP! CLAP!

I FEEL LIKE CELEBRATING. QUICK . . . PREPARE A FEAST! I WANT DELICIOUS FOOD AND DANCING.

AT ONCE, MY LORD!

THANK YOU, MY LORD!

DROOL

A TOAST TO OFFERUS!

CHEERS!

THIS IS YOUR ROOM, OFFERUS. HAVE A GOOD NIGHT.

WOW! LOOK AT THAT AWESOME BED!

LEAP!

BOOM!

OH NO . . . EARTHQUAKE!

SHAKE

SHAKE

BACK IN OFFERUS' HOMETOWN

HI, HELENA!

HAVE YOU HEARD FROM OFFERUS?

NO, NOT YET.

WHY DO YOU THINK HE LEFT WITHOUT SAYING GOODBYE?

I THINK IT WAS VERY SELFISH. HIS FATHER MISSES HIM.

OFFERUS, WHEREVER YOU ARE, I PRAY THAT GOD WILL HELP YOU FIND THE TRUTH.

HELENA . . .

I WONDER HOW SHE'S DOING . . . AND MY FAMILY. I MISS THEM.

OFFERUS, THE KING IS LOOKING FOR YOU.

OFFERUS WAS NOW THE KING'S BODYGUARD.

LET'S GO. I WANT TO TRAVEL AMONG THE PEOPLE.

THE KING EXTENDED HIS KINGDOM WITH OFFERUS BY HIS SIDE AS HIS LOYAL SERVANT.

THE KING'S WEALTH AND POWER INCREASED WITHOUT HIM HAVING TO DO ANY WORK.

DIE! YOU LIVE IN LUXURY OFF THE BACKS OF YOUR CITIZENS! WE STRUGGLE AND YOU HAVE WEALTH TO SPARE! DIE!

SOMETIMES ASSASSINS WOULD ATTACK THE KING, BUT . . .

SWOOSH

LEAVE AT ONCE AND I WILL LET YOU LIVE. WHAT DO YOU WANT TO DO?

JUST KILL HIM!

WITH OFFERUS AS HIS BODYGUARD, NO ONE WAS ABLE TO HARM THE KING.

I MADE THE RIGHT CHOICE IN MAKING YOU MY SERVANT. I AM SAFE WITH YOU NEXT TO ME.

BUT I DON'T LIKE THE FACT THAT YOU DIDN'T KILL HIM.

THANK YOU, MY LORD.

THE KING OFTEN REWARDED OFFERUS WITH EXPENSIVE GIFTS.

THIS DIAMOND IS YOURS!

WHOA!

I'M HAVING A HUGE PARTY FOR YOU, OFFERUS. YOU SAVED MY LIFE!

OFFERUS LIVED A COMFORTABLE LIFE, BUT HE FELT SAD.

I MISS HELENA AND MY FAMILY.

PARTY TIME! ♪ ♪
PARTY TIME! ♪

I KNOW! I'LL ASK THE KING IF MY FAMILY CAN LIVE HERE WITH ME.

MAYBE HELENA WOULD COME TOO.

OFFERUS! WHAT ARE YOU DOING OUT HERE? YOU'RE THE GUEST OF HONOR!

UMM... JUST NEED SOME FRESH AIR.

WOULD SHE MOVE HERE FOR ME?

OFFERUS, OFFERUS... DO YOU KNOW HOW MUCH I LOVE YOU?

HELENA! I MISS YOU. I HOPE WE MEET AGAIN SOON.

OFFERUS! WILL YOU DANCE WITH ME?

MONTHS LATER, AT THE KING'S BIRTHDAY PARTY

♪ HAPPY BIRTHDAY ♪♪ TO YOU!

THE KING IS REALLY HAPPY. THIS MIGHT BE THE BEST TIME TO ASK FOR MY FAMILY TO COME.

HERE COMES ANOTHER OF THE KING'S SERVANTS.

YOUR MAJESTY, HAPPY BIRTHDAY!

OH, YOU BROUGHT ME A GIFT! HOW KIND OF YOU!

OFFERUS, WHAT PRESENT DID YOU BRING?

HUH? I DIDN'T BRING HIM ANYTHING! WHAT SHOULD I DO?

HAHAHA! DON'T WORRY. YOUR SERVICE IS GIFT ENOUGH FOR HIM.

OH MAN . . .

I ONLY THOUGHT OF MYSELF. I SHOULD'VE BROUGHT A GIFT.

DO YOU KNOW HOW MUCH YOU HURT ME WHEN YOU THREW ME AGAINST THAT TREE?

MY KING, THE ROYAL POET WOULD LIKE TO READ A POEM WRITTEN IN YOUR HONOR.

GREAT KING OF CANAAN, I MUST TELL YOU—YOUR WEALTH IS SO WIDE IT ABOUNDS,

YOU WROTE A POEM FOR ME? LET'S HEAR IT.

THE KING IS AFRAID OF THE DEVIL?
I THOUGHT HE WAS THE MOST
POWERFUL MASTER!

CREAK
끼이익

WAKE UP, MY KING!

IT'S EARLY, MAXIMUS! WHAT DO YOU WANT?

YOUR SERVANT OFFERUS HAS GONE.

WHAT?

벌
SPROING!
떡

I FOUND THIS LETTER IN HIS ROOM.

SNATCH

타

OH MY. . .

CHAPTER 3

SEARCHING FOR THE DEVIL

IT'S REALLY HOT.
THE SUN IS SO
STRONG . . .

I CAN BARELY . . .
    B-BREATHE.

THUMP

I . . . MUST . . . KEEP
    . . . GOING . . .

UHH . . . A SHADOW?

WHAT ARE YOU DOING OUT HERE IN THE DESERT?

WHAA . . . WHO IS THIS KID?

IS THIS CHILD REAL? I MUST BE HALLUCINATING.

ARE YOU TRYING TO GET A SUNTAN?

PANT

GASP

BECAUSE I'M THE DEVIL.

HAHAHA

HAHAHAHAHAHA

SIGH

YOU THINK I'M JOKING?

LOOK, I HAVE NO IDEA WHY YOU'RE HERE. IF YOU HAVE SOME WATER YOU CAN SHARE, GREAT. OTHERWISE, GET LOST.

I AM THE DEVIL!

LISTEN, KID, I'M NOT THE PERSON YOU WANT TO LIE TO.

I AM THE . . .

WHOOSH

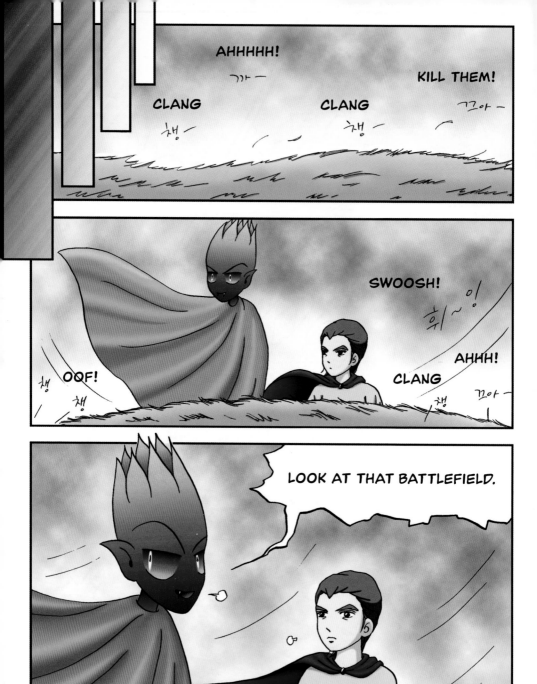

DID YOU HEAR THE RUMOR?

WHAT RUMOR?

THE DEVIL IS GETTING CLOSER TO OUR TOWN. HE WINS ALL OF HIS BATTLES. AND HE FILLS THE TOWNS WITH DISEASE AND TERRIBLE PLAGUES.

YES. I HEARD THAT THE DEVIL IS GROWING STRONGER AND HAS MANY FOLLOWERS.

IF OFFERUS WERE STILL HERE, OUR TOWN WOULD BE SAFE.

TRUE.

YOU KNOW, THERE'S A GREAT GIANT AMONG THE DEVIL'S FOLLOWERS . . .

DO YOU THINK OFFERUS IS . . .

SERVING THE DEVIL?

WELL . . . HE MIGHT BE.

ABSOLUTELY NOT! HE DOESN'T HURT PEOPLE.

WHAT IF THE DEVIL COMES TO OUR TOWN?

LET'S PRAY. PRAYER IS THE MOST POWERFUL WEAPON.

LORD, IF OFFERUS HAS DONE THIS, PLEASE SHOW HIM THE RIGHT WAY HE SHOULD FOLLOW.

HELENA . . .

IS HELENA YOUR GIRLFRIEND?

HUH!

WHAT? NO, SIR! I WAS JUST LOOKING AT THE MOON.

HUMAN BEINGS ARE SO WEAK. LOVE RUINS EVERYTHING. IT MAKES YOU WEAK. I THOUGHT YOU WERE STRONG, OFFERUS, BUT IT SEEMS YOU ARE LIKE EVERYONE ELSE.

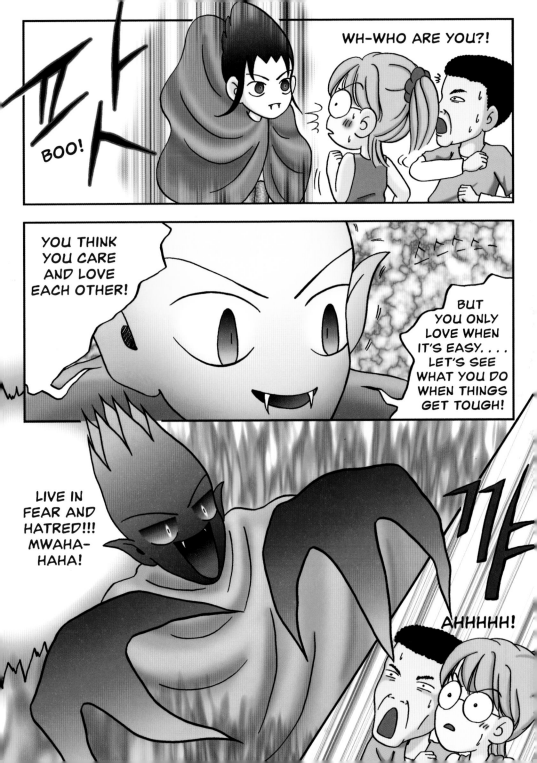

WHAT JUST HAPPENED?

JESUS SAVED US FROM THE DEVIL!

YOUR FACE PROBABLY SCARED HIM TOO! HEE HEE.

GRRR! WATCH WHAT YOU SAY, HUBBY!

I'M JUST KIDDING, SWEET-HEART.

LET'S CELEBRATE GOD'S VICTORY, A VICTORY FOR LOVE!

JESUS IS STRONGER THAN THE DEVIL!

WHY DID HE RUN AWAY LIKE THAT?

WAS THE DEVIL AFRAID OF THAT CROSS?

D-D-DID TH-TH-THEY L-L-LEAVE?

SHIVER

YEAH, THEY'RE GONE.

WHY WERE YOU AFRAID OF THAT CROSS?

GROWL

I AM NOT AFRAID OF THAT CROSS. IT'S JUST BAD LUCK.

I'VE GROWN TIRED OF THIS CONVERSATION. CHANGE THE TOPIC!

BUT I HAVE SOME QUESTIONS.

LIKE WHY ARE YOU SO SCARED OF THE CROSS? AND WHO IS JESUS?

CHANGE. THE. SUBJECT!

TELL ME.

FINE. I'LL TELL YOU BECAUSE YOU NEED TO KNOW ABOUT THIS DANGER TOO.

GO ON.

JESUS CHRIST DIED ON THE CROSS, ROSE FROM THE DEAD, AND SAVED THESE HUMANS! THAT'S WHY I BECOME WEAK WHEN I'M NEAR A CROSS.

SPIN

PLING!

ARRRGH! OFFERUS! I'LL NEVER FORGET THIS BETRAYAL, OFFERUS. YOU'LL BE CURSED FOR THE REST OF YOUR LIFE!

WOOSH

WOW! THE CROSS IS SO POWERFUL!

JESUS CHRIST. . . THAT'S HELENA'S GREAT KING! SHE WAS RIGHT. HE IS REAL. **JESUS** IS THE GREATEST KING.

CHAPTER
4

A NEW NAME

LOOKS LEFT

LOOKS RIGHT

LOOK AT THAT GIANT BEGGAR!

HE'S PROBABLY TRYING TO STEAL SOMETHING!

GET LOST, YOU DIRTY BEGGAR!

GET OUT OF OUR TOWN NOW!

PLINK!

PLONK!

CLONK

CLINK

YEAH! A DIRECT HIT!

I GOT HIM TOO!

UH-OH, THE GIANT LOOKS VERY ANGRY!

RUN! WE'D BETTER FIND HELP! WARN THE OTHERS!

UMM, EXCUSE ME. MAY I ASK YOU . . . ?

AAHH!!!! HELP! HE'S GOING TO HURT US!

HA! ME? A GIANT BEGGAR?

OH! I AM VERY DIRTY. NO WONDER THEY THOUGHT I WAS A BEGGAR!

SPLISH SPLASH

I HAVE BEEN LOOKING SO LONG FOR JESUS. WHERE CAN I FIND HIM?

PHEW! WHAT A LONG TRIP!

EWW! MY DIRTY FEET ARE IN THE WATER HE'S DRINKING!

GULP GULP

THANK YOU, LORD, FOR THIS WATER, BUT IT TASTES A LITTLE LIKE DIRTY FEET. HAHA!

SORRY . . .

GRAB

덥석

WHAT!? WHERE IS HE? HOW CAN I FIND HIM?

SHAKE!

LET ME GO AND I'LL TELL YOU!

JESUS DIED ON A CROSS SO THAT WE MIGHT LIVE! THE ONE TRUE GOD RAISED HIM FROM THE DEAD. HE LIVES IN EVERY BELIEVER. SO, JESUS IS RIGHT HERE IN MY HEART. I MEET HIM IN MY HEART EVERY DAY, EVERY HOUR, AND EVERY PLACE.

SO I'LL HAVE TO CUT HIM OUT OF YOUR HEART?!

NO! JESUS IS GOD, AND IF YOU BELIEVE IN HIM, HE'LL COME TO YOU.

SO . . .

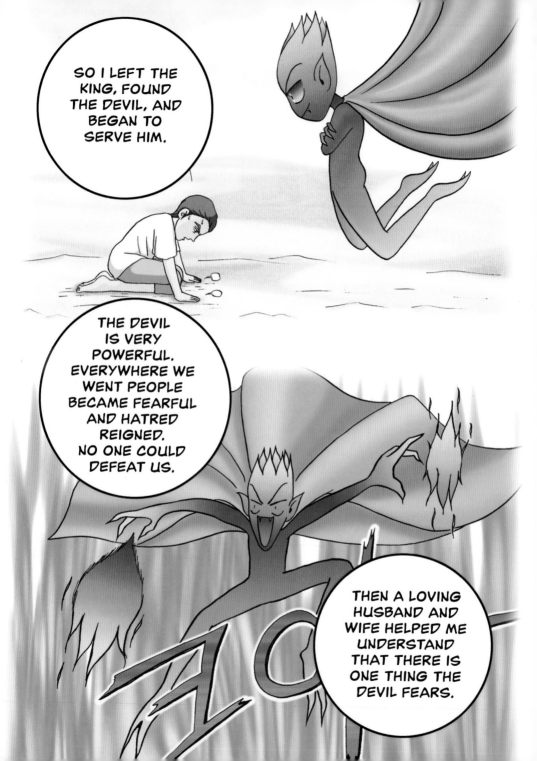

REALLY? WHAT MAKES THAT NASTY DEVIL RUN AWAY?

IT'S . . .

THE CROSS.

PRAISE THE LORD!

SOMETHING SO SIMPLE SCARED THE DEVIL.

THE DEVIL RAN TO AVOID THE LITTLE WOODEN CROSS THE WIFE HELD IN FRONT OF HIM. HE DID NOT TOUCH A HAIR ON HER HEAD.

JESUS MUST TRULY BE THIS GREAT KING I HAVE WANTED TO SERVE FOR MY ENTIRE LIFE. HE DIED ON THE CROSS AND ROSE FROM THE DEAD. NOW ANY LITTLE CROSS CAN DEFEAT THE DEVIL. I WANT TO BE THIS GREAT KING'S SERVANT.

SO, THAT'S WHY I WANT TO MEET JESUS.

OH! SO YOU WERE THE DEVIL'S RIGHT HAND MAN?

YES, I'M SO ASHAMED OF ALL I DID FOR HIM.

AFTER I LEFT THE DEVIL TO SEARCH FOR JESUS, I REALIZED THAT I HAD DONE MANY WRONG THINGS.

I JUST WANTED TO SERVE THE STRONGEST. INSTEAD, I HURT MANY PEOPLE WHEN I SERVED THE KING AND THE DEVIL.

WAAH!

HELP ME!!

FIRE!!

I WISH I COULD BE FORGIVEN FOR WHAT I DID. BUT HOW CAN SOMEONE LIKE ME BE FORGIVEN?

WHILE LOOKING FOR JESUS, I HAVE HEARD PEOPLE SAY THAT JESUS FORGIVES PEOPLE AND FREES THEM OF THEIR SIN. WOULD HE DO THAT FOR ME?

OFFERUS, ARE YOU TRULY SORRY FOR WHAT YOU DID?

NOD

THEN, JESUS WILL HAPPILY FORGIVE YOU.

JESUS IS GOD AND THE KING OF HEAVEN AND EARTH. YOU CAN BE HIS SERVANT. ANYONE WHO BELIEVES IN HIM CAN BE HIS SERVANT.

WHEN AND WHERE CAN I MEET HIM?

PRAY, DO GOOD, AND HAVE FAITH. THEN JESUS WILL COME TO YOU.

UMMM . . .

I DON'T KNOW HOW TO DO ANY OF THOSE THINGS.

GOD DOESN'T EXPECT YOU TO BE PERFECT. HE EXPECTS YOU TO TRY.

WHEN YOU SERVED THE DEVIL YOU HURT PEOPLE. NOW YOU CAN DO GOOD.

YOU COULD HELP THE PEOPLE WHO NEED TO REACH THE OTHER SIDE.

BECAUSE OF YOUR HEIGHT AND STRENGTH, OFFERUS, YOU COULD HELP THEM GET THERE SAFELY.

JESUS TOLD HIS FOLLOWERS TO LOVE EACH OTHER; HELPING OTHERS IS LOVING THEM.

IF I DO THIS, WILL I MEET JESUS?

JESUS ALSO TOLD US WHEN WE DO SOMETHING FOR SOMEONE IN NEED, WE'RE SERVING JESUS HIMSELF.

GREAT! I WANT TO SERVE JESUS SO I'LL START RIGHT AWAY!

HAHAHA! YOU DON'T HAVE TO BE IN SUCH A HURRY.

BUT I'VE BEEN SEARCHING FOR HIM FOR SO LONG SO I COULD SERVE HIM.

YOU BECAME HIS SERVANT WHEN YOU DESIRED FORGIVENESS AND BEGAN TO SEARCH FOR HIM.

REALLY?

IF YOU REALLY BELIEVE THAT JESUS IS GOD, THEN I CAN BAPTIZE YOU AND GIVE YOU A NEW NAME. ALL YOUR SINS WILL BE FORGIVEN AND YOU'LL BE BORN AGAIN IN JESUS CHRIST.

FORGIVEN AND REBORN?

YES, PLEASE BAPTIZE ME!

SPLASH, WOOSH

EVERYTHING I TOLD YOU ABOUT JESUS IS TRUE. I JUST ALSO HAPPEN TO NEED TO GET ACROSS.

DON'T LET ANGER PREVENT YOU FROM DOING GOOD. AND YOU MIGHT MAKE SOME MISTAKES THE FIRST TIME CROSSING THE RIVER.

THIS WILL BE A "PRACTICE RUN."

WHY IS THIS LITTLE MAN NOT WORRIED? THIS IS DANGEROUS!

DON'T WORRY. GOD WILL BE WITH US!

DOES JESUS MAKE HIM BRAVE?

I'LL SHARE MY SNACK WITH YOU

OK, TIME TO GO. JESUS WILL WATCH OVER US!

THUMPS CHEST

IS THIS THE STRENGTH JESUS GIVES?

WOW, CHRISTOPHER! IF I TRIED WADING ACROSS, I WOULD DROWN!

HAHAHA!

HUSH, OR I MIGHT LOSE MY GRIP AND DROP YOU!

하하하

HㅑHOHOHOH — RUSHING WATER

UMM... WHAT'S THAT NOISE?

CRASH!

ㅐㅑㅐ이이이아!

WAIT HERE. I'LL GO GET YOUR HORSE NEXT.

NO, IT'S OK. I'LL LEAVE HIM THERE.

HEY!

THANKS MUCH. MAY GOD BLESS YOU FOR HELPING ME!

I'M GLAD TO HAVE BEEN OF SERVICE.

CHRISTOPHER, I'LL ALWAYS PRAY FOR YOU. CONTINUE TO LOVE GOD BY HELPING OTHERS.

I WANT TO GIVE YOU THIS CROSS I HAVE WORN FOR YEARS. MAY YOU REMEMBER THAT JESUS IS WITH YOU ALWAYS!

THANK YOU, FATHER!

BYE!

THE RIVER OF DEATH. NOT EASY TO CROSS, BUT . . .

I'LL DO IT FOR JESUS. I'LL HELP THE PEOPLE ACROSS!

OUCH!

WHAT'S THIS? SOMEONE COULD GET HURT, SOMEONE LIKE ME.

BOY, THAT HURT!

CHAPTER 5

WEIGHT OF THE WORLD

HEY, BUDDY! LET GO OF MY BOAT RIGHT NOW! I'VE GOT PLACES TO GO!

I'M TRYING TO HELP YOU. IF YOU CROSS IN THIS LITTLE BOAT, IT'LL CAPSIZE AND YOU'LL DIE.

I KNOW HOW TO ROW A BOAT! I NEED TO GET ACROSS NOW!

MY DAD'S ACROSS THE RIVER AND HE'S REALLY SICK. IF I TAKE THE LONG WAY THERE, I MAY ARRIVE TOO LATE. NOW, LET ME GO!

I UNDERSTAND. BUT GET OUT OF THE BOAT FIRST.

DIDN'T YOU HEAR ME?!

YOU BULLY!! YOU PROBABLY WANT ME TO PAY YOU TO CROSS!

I'M NOT GETTING OUT!

GRAB

GRAB

FLOP 첨

DON'T WORRY. I'LL HELP YOU ACROSS SO YOU CAN SEE YOUR DAD. I'LL KEEP YOU SAFE.

WHAT'RE YOU DOING? WHERE'S YOUR BOAT?

WE'LL BE FINE. CLOSE YOUR EYES IF YOU'RE SCARED.

질끈

SQUEEZE.

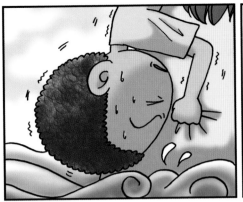

OKAY, WE'RE HERE!

HUH? REALLY?

I APOLO-GIZE FOR SCARING YOU, SIR.

H-H-HOW DID YOU GET US ACROSS THIS QUICKLY?

THE RIVER IS QUIET TODAY. I THINK JESUS IS DOING IT SO YOU CAN SEE YOUR DAD.

BUT . . . WITH-OUT A BOAT?

하하하

HEE HEE

SWISH SWOSH

WILL YOU BE ABLE TO HELP ME ON THE WAY BACK, CHRISTOPHER?

HAHAHA. YES, OF COURSE!

WOW! I FEEL SO HAPPY. I NEVER FELT THIS WAY WHEN I SERVED THE KING OR THE DEVIL.

GOD HAS FILLED ME WITH JOY AND PEACE BECAUSE I'M SERVING HIM BY HELPING OTHERS.

IT FEELS LIKE WHEN I USED TO HELP PEOPLE AT HOME. OH . . .

HELENA.

SWISH SWOSH

HI, CHRISTOPHER!

REMEMBER ME?

OF COURSE!

HOW'S YOUR DAD?

HE'S GREAT NOW. I GOT THERE IN TIME TO GET HIM TO A DOCTOR!

YOU'RE A GOOD SON.

UMM . . . I'M SORRY TO ASK, BUT . . .

YOU NEED TO CROSS THE RIVER?

WOULD YOU MIND?

OF COURSE NOT!

THANK YOU SO MUCH! THANK YOU!

YOU'VE THANKED ME ENOUGH. LET'S GO!

HEY, WHAT ARE YOU WAITING FOR?

WELL . . . YOU SEE . . . IT'S NOT JUST ME THAT HAS TO CROSS.

WAIT A MOMENT!

HERE THEY ARE!

THESE PEOPLE WERE FORCED TO LEAVE THEIR HOMES BECAUSE OF WAR.

THEY HAVE TO GET TO THE OTHER SIDE OF THE RIVER BEFORE THEY ARE CAPTURED.

IF OUR ENEMIES FIND US, THEY'LL ENSLAVE OUR CHILDREN

AND KILL THE REST OF US.

SOB

CHRISTOPHER, CAN YOU HELP THEM TOO?

WELL, I CAN'T CARRY THEM ALL AT ONCE—

PLEASE, JUST SAVE OUR CHILDREN. WE'LL GO AROUND THE RIVER!

RIGHT. OKAY, KIDS, LET'S GO.

NO, WE DON'T WANT TO LEAVE YOU! I'M SCARED.

IT'S ALRIGHT. IT WILL BE FINE. MOM AND I WILL GO AROUND THE RIVER.

THIS MAN WILL KEEP YOU SAFE. WE'LL SEE YOU SOON. BE GOOD.

YOU MUST GO.

SOB WAAH

WE HAVE TO HURRY SO WE CAN MEET THE CHILDREN.

JUST WAIT THERE. I'LL COME BACK AND GET YOU AS SOON AS I CAN!

I KNEW CHRISTOPHER WOULD HELP ALL OF YOU!

HAHA! WHAT DID I TELL YOU? HE'S A BLESSING, A GIFT FROM GOD!

YES, YES. THANK YOU SO MUCH!

CHRISTOPHER MUST BE AN ANGEL FROM HEAVEN.

ㅊㄹㅈ/% WOOSH

ㅋㅈ/% CRASH

AFTER CARRYING THE CHILDREN, HE RETURNED FOR THE ADULTS—

FIRST THE GRANDMOTHER . . .

BOOM

THEN THE PARENTS.

HOLD ON TIGHT, HONEY!

I WISH I WERE IN THE MIDDLE.

HMM . . .

WITH GOD'S HELP, I CAN DO THIS!

HELENA, I WISH YOU COULD SEE ME . . .

HOLD ON TIGHT OR YOU'LL FALL.

WAHOO! THIS IS AWESOME!

YOU WOULD BE SURPRISED TO SEE . . .

EVERY DAY I HELP PEOPLE CROSS THE RIVER BECAUSE OF MY KING, JESUS CHRIST.

쇼아ОН CRASH

ОН ОН ОН

BOOM

THANK YOU, JESUS, FOR FINDING ME AND FOR NEVER LEAVING ME ALONE.

I WILL SERVE YOU FOREVER.

ONE NIGHT . . .

PLEASE HELP ME!

HUH?
WHAT?

WOOSHH

WOOO

THAT'S JUST
THE WIND. I MUST
HAVE BEEN
DREAMING . . .

PLEASE HELP ME!

WHAT?

DO I HEAR A CHILD?

WOW, THAT DREAM WAS SO REAL.

WHO'S THERE?

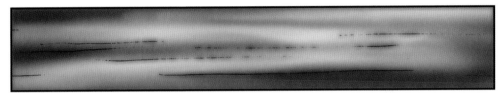

A BABY . . . OUT HERE IN THE MIDDLE OF THE NIGHT?

CHRISTOPHER, WON'T YOU TAKE ME ACROSS THE RIVER?

YOU CAN TALK? AND WHAT ARE YOU DOING HERE ALL ALONE?

PLEASE.

OK, KID. IT'S LATE SO I'LL TAKE YOU TOMORROW MORNING.

I CAN'T WAIT. PLEASE TAKE ME NOW.

WHO IS THIS?

위이~
BEGONE

BEGONE?

HE DIDN'T RUN AWAY, SO HE CAN'T BE THE DEVIL.

I WON'T GO AWAY.

THERE IS SOMETHING SO DIFFERENT ABOUT THIS BABY.

HE IS SO CALM, AND HIS FACE IS AS BRIGHT AS THE MOON.

SORRY FOR DOUBTING YOU. THE CURRENT ISN'T TOO BAD, SO I THINK WE CAN MAKE IT ACROSS SAFELY.

DON'T WORRY, LITTLE ONE. I'LL KEEP YOU SAFE.

LIFT

I'VE TIED YOU ON PRETTY WELL, BUT HOLD ON TIGHT ANYWAY.

WHO IS THIS TALKING BABY WHO NEEDS TO CROSS THE RIVER AT NIGHT? THIS IS VERY STRANGE.

WHAT'S EVEN STRANGER IS THAT I AGREED TO DO IT!

STILL, I'M GLAD TO LOVE AND SERVE IN JESUS' NAME.

WHEW! IT FEELS LIKE THIS BABY IS GETTING HEAVIER!

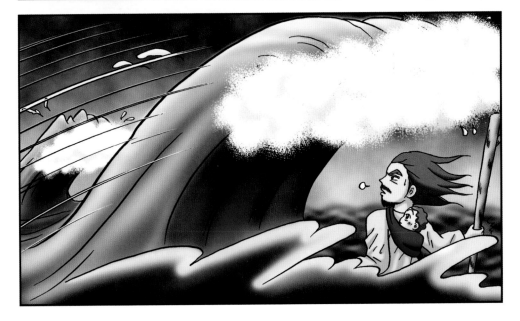

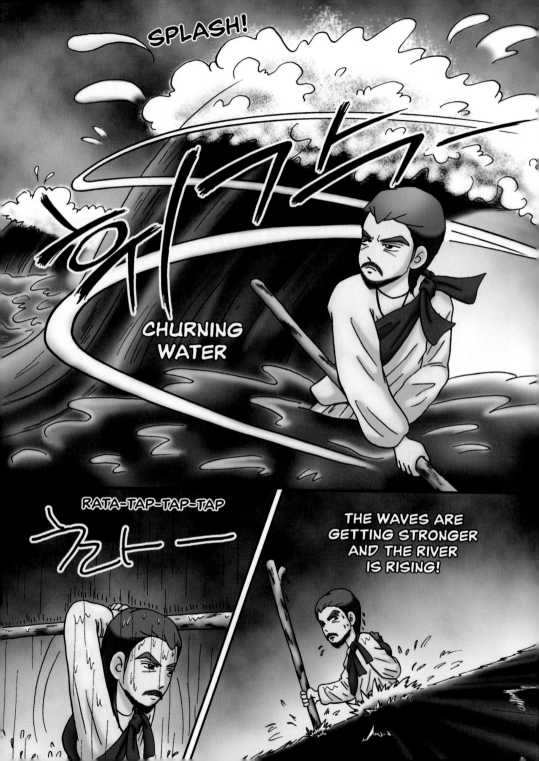

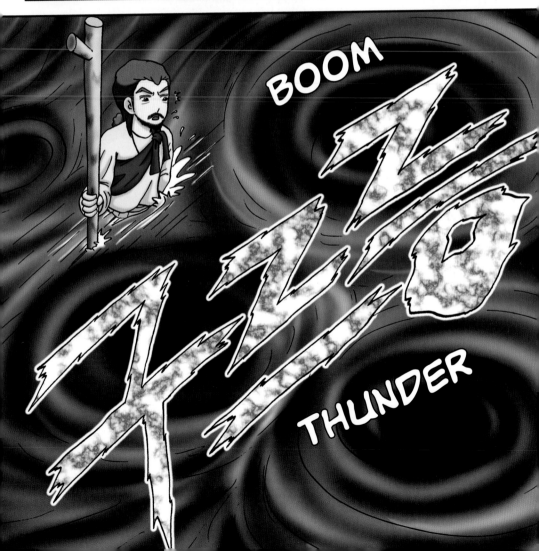

WOBBLE!

ARGHH! THE CURRENT!

IT'S NEVER BEEN SO HARD BEFORE TO CROSS THE RIVER. JESUS, PLEASE HELP ME KEEP THIS CHILD SAFE!

I DON'T KNOW HOW MUCH LONGER I CAN CARRY HIM. MY GOD, I'VE ALWAYS RELIED ON MY OWN STRENGTH, BUT I NEED YOU TO HELP ME!

YOU SCARED ME! I THOUGHT I HAD LOST YOU.

PHEW!

ARE YOU SCARED? COME HERE. I'LL TAKE YOU WHERE YOU NEED TO GO.

CHRISTOPHER!

YOU CROSSED THE RIVER NOT ONLY WITH THE WEIGHT OF THE WORLD ON YOUR BACK, BUT HIM WHO MADE THE WORLD!

HUH? WHAT?

YOU PROTECTED ME.

HE'S ALMOST GLOWING.

IS THIS BABY . . . ?

COULD IT BE . . . ?

RUSTLE

TWITCH

WIGGLE

WIGGLE

SPROING

SPROING

WITNESS AND SERVANT TO JESUS CHRIST

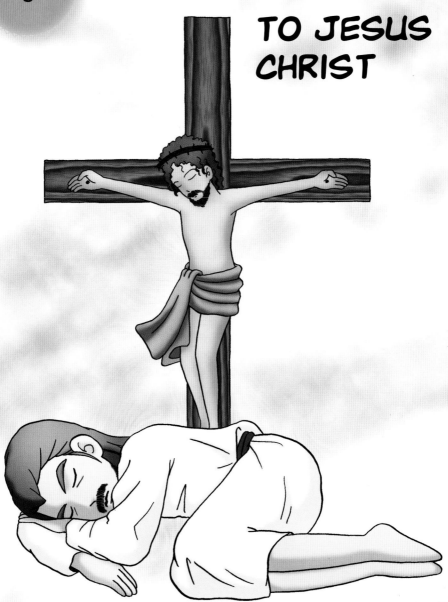

옹성
GRUMBLE

옹성
MUTTER

CHRISTOPHER'S WALKING STICK BECAME A TREE.

HOW DID THAT HAPPEN?

JESUS DID THIS MIRACLE.

JESUS MUST HAVE QUIETED THE RIVER, TOO.

I WONDER IF I WOULD BECOME LIKE CHRISTOPHER IF I ATE SOME FRUIT.

HA! YOU WOULDN'T BE LIKE HIM IF YOU ATE THE WHOLE TREE!

CHRISTOPHER!

HEY!

GO AHEAD. EAT THE FRUIT. YOU'LL STILL JUST BE YOU!

LET'S PRAY TOGETHER.

TEACH US MORE ABOUT JESUS, CHRISTOPHER!

YES, LET'S!

THE PALACE IN LYCIA.

HAVE YOU HEARD OF THIS MAN CALLED CHRISTOPHER?

YEAH, EVERYONE IS TALKING ABOUT HIM.

HE USED TO HELP PEOPLE CROSS A DANGEROUS RIVER. BUT NOW HE GOES EVERYWHERE PREACHING ABOUT JESUS.

THE PEOPLE LOVE HIM. CROWDS GATHER TO LISTEN TO HIM TALK ABOUT HIS GREAT KING: JESUS CHRIST.

HOW DARE HE CHALLENGE OUR KING'S AUTHORITY! WE HAVE TO STOP CHRISTOPHER.

WE'LL HAVE TO CAPTURE HIM TO STOP HIM.

IT WON'T BE EASY. HE'S SO TALL AND STRONG.

BUT WE'VE GOT TO STOP HIM, AT ANY COST! WE CAN'T LET HIM KEEP PREACHING LIKE THAT!

I CAN GET HIM!

TRUST ME, MY LORD. I'LL MAKE THAT GIANT KNEEL IN FRONT OF YOU!

GOOD, CAPTURE HIM FOR ME AT ONCE!

BUT BRING HIM TO ME ALIVE. I WANT TO ASK HIM SOMETHING FIRST.

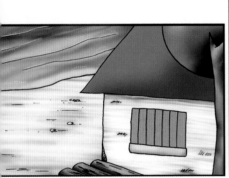

CHRISTOPHER! PLEASE, I NEED YOUR HELP.

HOW CAN I HELP YOU?

MY WIFE HAS SLIPPED AND IS HANGING OFF THE CLIFF. ONLY YOU CAN HELP SAVE HER!

OF COURSE! WHERE IS SHE?

SHE'S OVER THERE.

POOR CHRISTOPHER! LIKE A TRAPPED RAT. YOU'VE GROWN SOFT, ALWAYS TRYING TO HELP PEOPLE.

FOOTSTEPS

WHO ARE YOU?!

ME? I'M YOUR CAPTOR!

WHY ARE YOU DOING THIS?

YOU'RE DONE, CHRISTOPHER.

....

DO YOU LIKE THE METAL NET I HAD MADE ESPECIALLY FOR YOU?

YOU WON'T BE ABLE TO BREAK IT!

CLINK

I DON'T NEED TO BREAK IT. I CAN JUST TOSS IT!

IF YOU JUST LEAVE, YOU'LL BE FINE!

I KNEW THIS MIGHT HAPPEN.

THE NET WAS JUST FOR FUN. I KNOW HOW TO MAKE YOU COME WITH ME.

TA-DA!

CHRISTOPHER, HELP!

YOU'LL COME OF YOUR OWN FREE WILL.

THESE SOLDIERS WILL KILL YOUR FRIENDS IF YOU TRY ANYTHING.

WHAT DO YOU WANT FROM ME?

COME WITH ME QUIETLY.

D-DON'T LET THEM KILL ME.

SOB SOB

FINE. LET THEM GO AND I'LL GO WITH YOU.

I'LL DO AS YOU SAY.

I'LL LET THEM GO AS SOON AS I'VE DELIVERED YOU TO THE PALACE.

HEY, I THOUGHT WE HAD A DEAL!

AHHH!

IF YOU KILL HIM YOU'LL REGRET IT!

I HATE BLOOD-SHED AS MUCH AS MOST PEOPLE.

BUT THESE SOLDIERS LOVE TO MAKE PEOPLE BLEED.

GIVE UP AND COME WITH ME. IT'S THE ONLY WAY THEY'LL STAY ALIVE.

FINE. BUT KEEP . . .

YOUR PROMISE!

I'LL GO.

털썩!

THE KING'S PALACE

SO YOU'RE THE ONE WHO TELLS PEOPLE TO FOLLOW ANOTHER KING.

I MEAN NO DISRESPECT TO YOU, BUT THE PEOPLE DESERVE TO KNOW THE TRUTH.

THE PEOPLE FOLLOW JESUS CHRIST, THE KING OF THE WORLD!

THE KING OF THE WORLD?

YES.

WHO IS THE KING?

JESUS CHRIST IS THE GREATEST KING!

TORTURE HIM UNTIL HE ADMITS I AM THE ONLY KING.

HOW DARE YOU!

YES, SIR!

SUPER HOT CHILIES!

YOU'VE BEEN HERE FOR A WHILE. YOU MUST BE HUNGRY. OPEN WIDE. I HAVE A TREAT FOR YOU!

EAT THESE OR I'LL SEND THE SOLDIERS TO KILL THE VILLAGERS!

MMPH!

WHO IS THE MOST POWERFUL KING IN THE WORLD NOW?

JESUS. . . . IT WILL ALWAYS BE JESUS. . . . HE HAS LOVED AND FORGIVEN ME. HE IS THE GREATEST.

YOU STUBBORN MAN! I KNOW HOW TO CHANGE YOUR MIND.

LET'S SEE IF YOUR KING SAVES YOU FROM FIRE.

CHATTER

OH, NO! IT'S CHRISTOPHER!

PLEASE DON'T!

WHY WOULD THEY HURT HIM?

CAN'T WE HELP HIM?

STOP THEM!

GO!

START THE FIRE!

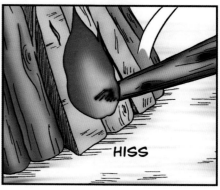

HISS

CRACKLE

NO!! CHRISTOPHER!!

WOW!

FIZZLE

CHRISTOPHER IS SAFE! IT'S A MIRACLE!

GOD SENT THE RAIN TO PUT OUT THE FIRE!

NOTHING IS IMPOSSIBLE FOR GOD!

JESUS SAVED HIM FROM BEING BURNT ALIVE!

IT'S ANOTHER MIRACLE!

HOW IS THIS POSSIBLE? GRRRR.

DO YOU HAVE ANY LAST WORDS, TRAITOR?

LET'S END THIS NOW. JUST KILL HIM!

HE HAS DONE NO WRONG!

FREE HIM! FREE HIM!

IS THAT YOU, HELENA?

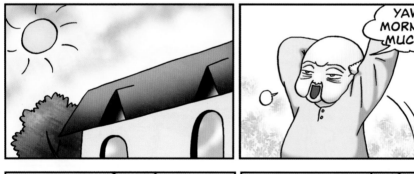

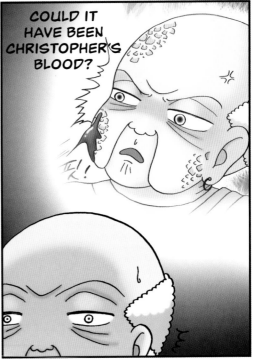

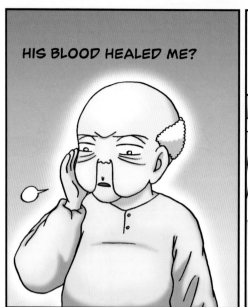

CHRISTOPHER KNEW THAT JESUS IS THE KING OF THE WORLD. I WILL FOLLOW JESUS CHRIST LIKE HE DID.

I'M IN HEAVEN PRAYING
FOR ALL OF YOU,

AND JESUS ALWAYS LISTENS TO
OUR PRAYERS!

MAY GOD BLESS ALL OF
YOUR TRAVELS!

—HYOUN-JU LEE,
AUTHOR

Courage

Commitment

Compassion

These are just some of the qualities of the saints you'll find in our popular Encounter the Saints series. Join Saint John Neumann, Saint Clare of Assisi, Saint Francis of Assisi, and many other holy men and women as they discover and try to do what God asks of them. Get swept into the exciting and inspiring lives of the Church's heroes and heroines while encountering the saints in a new and fun way!

Collect all the Encounter the Saints books by visiting www.pauline.org/ EncountertheSaints

Saint John Neumann

Missionary to Immigrants

Laura Rhoderica Brown, FSP

ENCOUNTER THE SAINTS SERIES

Saint Clare of Assisi

A Light for the World

by Marianne Lorraine Trouve, FSP

Saint Francis of Assisi

Gentle Revolutionary

by Mary Emmanuel Alves, FSP

Who are the
Daughters of St. Paul?

We are Catholic sisters with a mission. Our task is to bring the love of Jesus to everyone like Saint Paul did. You can find us in over 50 countries. Our founder, Blessed James Alberione, showed us how to reach out to the world through the media. That's why we publish books, make movies and apps, record music, broadcast on radio, perform concerts, help people at our bookstores, visit parishes, host JClub book fairs, use social media and the Internet, and pray for all of you.

Visit our Web site at www.pauline.org

Pauline
BOOKS & MEDIA

The Daughters of St. Paul operate book and media centers at the following addresses. Visit, call, or write the one nearest you today, or find us at www.paulinestore.org.

CALIFORNIA
3908 Sepulveda Blvd, Culver City, CA 90230 — 310-397-8676
3250 Middlefield Road, Menlo Park, CA 94025 — 650-369-4230

FLORIDA
145 SW 107th Avenue, Miami, FL 33174 — 305-559-6715

HAWAII
1143 Bishop Street, Honolulu, HI 96813 — 808-521-2731

ILLINOIS
172 North Michigan Avenue, Chicago, IL 60601 — 312-346-4228

LOUISIANA
4403 Veterans Memorial Blvd, Metairie, LA 70006 — 504-887-7631

MASSACHUSETTS
885 Providence Hwy, Dedham, MA 02026 — 781-326-5385

MISSOURI
9804 Watson Road, St. Louis, MO 63126 — 314-965-3512

NEW YORK
64 West 38th Street, New York, NY 10018 — 212-754-1110

SOUTH CAROLINA
243 King Street, Charleston, SC 29401 — 843-577-0175

TEXAS—Currently no book center; for parish exhibits or outreach evangelization, contact: 210-569-0500 or SanAntonio@paulinemedia.com or P.O. Box 761416, San Antonio, TX 78245

VIRGINIA
1025 King Street, Alexandria, VA 22314 — 703-549-3806

CANADA
3022 Dufferin Street, Toronto, ON M6B 3T5 — 416-781-9131

SMILE God loves you